Aphorisms of Yôga

also translated by Shree Purohit Swāmi

THE TEN PRINCIPAL UPANISHADS
(*with W. B. Yeats*)

THE GEETĀ

Aphorisms of Yôga
by
Bhagwān Shree Patanjali

*done into English
from the original in Samskrit
with a commentary
by*

Shree Purohit Swāmi

*and an introduction
by*

W. B. Yeats

FABER AND FABER
3 Queen Square
London

First published in June 1938
This edition first published in 1973
by Faber and Faber Limited
3 Queen Square London W.C.1
Reprinted 1975
Printed in Great Britain by
Whitstable Litho Ltd., Whitstable, Kent
All rights reserved

ISBN 0 571 10320 0

In gratefulness
to my Master
Bhagwān Shree Hamsa
at whose feet
I sat and learnt

Contents

Introduction

I

Some years ago I bought *The Yôga-System of Patanjali*, translated and edited by James Horton Woods and published by the Harvard Press. It is the standard edition, final, impeccable in scholastic eyes, even in the eyes of a famous poet and student of Samskrit, who used it as a dictionary. But then the poet was at his university, but lately out of school, had not learned to hate all scholar's cant and class-room slang, nor was he an old man in a hurry.

Certainly before the Ajantā Caverns were painted, almost certainly before the ribbed dome and bell columns of Kārli were carved, naked ascetics had put what they believed an ancient wisdom into short aphorisms for their pupils to get by heart and put in practice. I come in my turn, no grammarian, but a man engaged in that endless research into life, death, God, that is every man's revery. I want to hear the talk of those naked men, and I am certain they never said 'The subliminal impression produced this (super repetive balanced state)' nor talked of 'predicate relations'. Then I found among some typed papers on various subjects a first draft of Shree Purohit Swāmi's translation and was moderately content. A little later he said he was engaged on a commentary, and when we had finished *The Ten Principal Upanishads* he began to read it out. Now and then I would stop him to simplify or condense a phrase, or to ask him this or that. He had practised certain meditations, had certain experiences described or implied by Patanjali, and as a Brāhman monk had encircled India for nine years. He knew what he wrote about, he knew it in his bones as no European scholar could, and now after a couple of years I re-read with excitement. With his consent I lent the manuscript to the only Indian scholar in my circle, and though her excitement was not less than mine she objected to the anecdotes, the personal experiences that seemed to her to break the logical tension. If they are a fault, the fault is mine, for I begged the Swāmi to be as anecdotal, biographical, as he could, because we know nothing of those who study and put in practice the Aphorisms of Patanjali.

II

Some scholars attribute the Aphorisms to a
certain Patanjali who lived in the second century B.C., others to a man of the same name
who lived in the third, fourth or fifth century
A.D.; others have held that these two men
were one man who lived at an unknown date.
All are agreed that he but recorded or systema-
tised an ancient knowledge. The most famous
of the commentaries were written apparently
between the third and the ninth centuries
A.D. Shree Purohit Swāmi has made some
use of them, and the more important are fully
translated by James Horton Woods.

III

In all civilisations comes a moment when
mass feeling and the dominant images that ex-
cite it weaken; when poetic certainty recedes
before doubt and analysis. In the *Brihadār-
anyaka-Upanishad* there is a certain Yādnyawalkya into whose mouth are put profound
thoughts, litanies, variations upon a theme:
'Thunder is the honey of all beings; all beings
the honey of thunder. The bright eternal Self
that is in thunder, the bright eternal Self that
lives in the voice, are one and the same; that is

13

immortality, that is Spirit, that is all.' He lived, according to some European scholars, about 600 B.C. before the composition of most of the Wedic Hymns, though Indian scholars put all these events much earlier. Like Pythagoras, who occupied the same place in Greek civilisation, he substituted philosophic reason for custom and mythology, put an end to the Golden Age and began that of the Sophists, an intellectual anarchy that found its Socrates in Buddha. He had substituted the eternal Self for all the gods.[1]

The little I know of India has come to me in the main by word of mouth. A man from Malabār described that age of the sophists, 'thought and action became ends in themselves, the forest Brāhmans, each with his group of students, thought of nothing but wrangling, the military caste in the towns thought of nothing but their military business. They would let out a horse and any town that stopped the horse had to fight. Buddha tried to put down both Brāhman and soldier, failed against the Brāhman, was too successful against the soldier for he destroyed our power of self-protection. We have been conquered by race after race, Syrian, Persian, French, English.'

[1] See *History of World Civilisations* by Hermann Schneider, translated by Marjorie Green, Vol. II, page 706.

IV

Somewhere in this Sophistic period came
Patanjali and his Aphorisms. Unlike Buddha
he turned from ordinary men; he sought truth
not by the logic or the moral precepts that
draw the crowd, but by methods of meditation
and contemplation that purify the soul. The
truth cannot be found by argument, the soul
itself is truth, it is that Self praised by Yādnyawalkya which is all Selves. The school of
Yādnyawalkya and its historical preparation
replaced the trance of the sôma drinkers (I
think of the mescal of certain Mexican tribes),
or that induced by beaten drums, or by cere-
monial dancing before the image of a god, by a
science that seems to me as reasonable as it
must have seemed to its first discoverer.
Through states analagous to self-induced hyp-
notic sleep the devotee attains a final state of
complete wakefulness called, now conscious
Samādhi, now Tureeyā, where the soul, puri-
fied of all that is not itself, comes into posses-
sion of its own timelessness. Matter, or the
soul's relation to time has disappeared; souls
that have found like freedom in the remote
past, or will find it in the future, enter into it or
are entered by it at will, nor is it bound to any
part of space, nor to any process, it depends

only upon itself, is Spirit, that which has value in itself.[1]

V

That experience, accessible to all who adopt a traditional technique and habit of life, has become the central experience of Indian civilisation, perhaps of all Far-Eastern civilisation, that wherein all thoughts and all emotions expect their satisfaction and rest. The technique in China and Japan is different, but not that experience. In the Upanishads and in Patanjali the Self and the One are reality. There are other books, Indian or Chinese, where the Self or the Not-Self, the One and the Many, are alike illusion. Whatever is known to the logical intellect is this and not that, here and not there, before and not after, or confined to one wing or another of some antinomy. It became no longer possible to identify the One and the Self with reality, the method of meditation had to be changed. Some years ago, that I might understand its influence upon Chinese

[1] To Aristotle and to Christian orthodoxy only God has value in Himself, even Spirit is contingent. At the fall of Hellenism and its exaltation of personality instinct demanded an extreme objectivity. Man had to annihilate himself. Spirit alone has value, Spirit has no value. Eternity expresses itself through contradictions.

16

and Japanese landscape painting, I sought that method in vain through encyclopedias and histories; it certainly prepared an escape from all that intellect holds true, and that escape, as described in the Scriptures and the legends of Zen Buddhism, is precipitated by shock, often produced artificially by the teacher. A young monk said to the Abbot, 'I have noticed that when anybody has asked about Nirwāna you merely raise your right hand and lower it again, and now when I am asked I answer in the same way.' The Abbot seized his hand and cut off a finger. The young monk ran away screaming, then stopped and looked back. The Abbot raised his hand and lowered it, and at that moment the young monk attained the supreme joy. 'No more does the young man come from behind the embroidered curtain amid the sweet clouds of incense; he goes among his friends, he goes among the flute players, something very nice has happened to the young man, but he can only tell it to his sweetheart.'

VI

Before Humanism, before the Renaissance, the popular intellect found rest and satisfaction in the adoration of God imagined as the figure on the Cross, or the Child upon its Mother's knee, but to the Humanist this must have seemed as alien as did the mythology of early India or Greece to the followers of Yād-nyawalkya or Pythagoras, but no Zen Buddhism, no Yôgi practice, no Neo-Platonic discipline, came to find a substitute. Our mechanical science intervened.

Goethe alone among men of genius has attempted to become wise, as the ancients understood that word. I who owed as much in youth to *Wilhelm Meister* as in later years to the *Comédie Humaine*, join in the general admiration. In *Faust* he sought to experience, and tried to express, a moment acceptable to reason where our thoughts and emotions could find satisfaction or rest. Faust, in the first part, refuses to say 'In the beginning was the Word', and substitutes 'In the beginning was the Act', and when at last he almost cries 'Stay Moment!' it is in contemplation of men struggling to save a small patch of cultivated land from inundation. He may have thought of nothing but his dislike for all abstract, or disembodied thought, of his conviction that culture (was that the cultivated land?) and its creation and defence was the only good, yet I think he meant more than that. He is vague, he does not cry 'Stay Moment!' but says that he might cry it, and there seems no reason for this distinction. Perhaps thought failed, as I think, his life failed, before what seemed the supreme test of his philosophy. He sought unity, that unity which Dante compared to a perfectly proportioned human body, and but turned from one occupation to another. As he approached what seemed to him success his poetry dissolved in abstraction and complexity. Had he died in 1800 *Faust*, including what was already written of the second part, would have remained, though fragmentary, a work of art throughout. Gentile, the Italian Hegelian philosopher, finds in those words of Faust a conviction that ultimate reality is the Pure Act, the actor and the thing acted upon, the puncher and the punching-ball, consumed away. If Goethe fàiled, he failed because neither he nor his audience knew of any science or philosophy that sought, not a change of opinion, but a different level of consciousness; knowing nothing of white heat he sought truth in the cold iron.

VII

In the seventeenth century conscious Samā-dhi re-appeared in the 'walking trance' of Boehme, when truth fell upon him 'like a bursting shower', and in the eighteenth, much contaminated by belief in the literal inspiration of Scripture, in the visions of Swedenborg. Possibly I should deny to the visions of Swedenborg, as I do to those of Saint Theresa who lived back somewhere near the basarid and the sôma drinker, the character of conscious Samādhi; conscious Samādhi, Tureeyā as Patanjali or the Upanishads understand that term is a sovereign condition and cannot accept a limit. 'You ask me what is my religion and I hit you upon the mouth,' wrote a Japanese monk upon attaining Nirwāna. But we may, I think, concede to Swedenborg an impure Samādhi. Boehme had great influence upon the theology of the seventeenth century and some on modern German philosophy; Swedenborg gave what there is of anatomy to the sentimental body of spiritualistic theory, but 'walking trance' and vision were themselves uninvestigated. In the first half of the nineteenth century French hypnotists, or as they were then called, mesmerists, investigated the Yôgi sleep from outside, discovering as they believed, a series of spiritual states from man to God, and were the first to study clairvoyance and fore-knowledge. From America in the middle of the century came the Yôga sleep of the spirit medium. So great had been the influence of the French hypnotists, largely, as I think, through the incorporation of their discoveries in the novels of Balzac, Dumas, Georges Sand, that there are two interpretations of psychic phenomena. In England and America it is attributed to spirits, whereas almost without exception, Continental investigators discover its origin in some hitherto unimagined power of the individual mind and body. These points of view, spiritism and animism, are not in the eyes of the student of Yôga contradictory; to quote the *Chāndôgya-Upanishad*, 'the wise man sees in Self those that are alive and those that are dead'.

W. B. YEATS

Dublin 1937

I
Illumination

I

Illumination

1. We now begin the exposition of yôga.

2. Yôga is controlling the activities of mind (chitta).

Chitta is mind as a whole, the mind-material.

The word yôga comes from yuja to join or yoke. It joins the personal Self and the impersonal Self.

When the three qualities of mind, purity passion ignorance, are controlled, the two Selves are yoked.

3. When mind is controlled, Self stays in His native condition.

4. Otherwise He conforms to the nature of mind's activities.

When mind is immovable, Self is like the sun when the clouds are gone, like the bottom of the lake when there are no ripples. It shows its true form.

But there is constant movement among the three qualities, sometimes purity prevails, at others passion or ignorance. Mind is controlled when it is withdrawn from movement; then the Self, which until then had identified itself with these, cannot identify itself with anything but itself.

5. The activities are five-fold; some painful, others pleasurable.

6. They are: experience, perversion, delusion, sleep, recollection.

7. Experience comes from perception, inference, evidence.

Perception is smelling, touching, tasting, seeing, hearing, but mind must be added before it becomes experience or knowledge.

8. Perversion is an idea of an object, not conforming to its nature.

We are in a hurry to come to a conclusion, we commit mistakes, think that mother-of-pearl is silver, a rubber snake a real snake.

9. Delusion is an idea conveyed by words, without any reality.

10. Sleep is a condition, which depends on the cessation of perception.

11. Recollection is the calling up of past experience.

All flights of imagination come from experience in past lives, stored up, it may be, for thousands of years.

12. Control the activities by practice and detachment.

13. Practice is effort towards concentration.

14. Long unremitting sincere practice develops into habit.

Lord Buddha took thirteen lives to attain illumination; Saint Bahinābāi in her autobiography describes the thirteen lives before she attained.

15. Detachment is the deliberate renunciation of desire for objects seen or heard.

Desirelessness brings liberation; the desire for liberation is no desire; it is the affirmation of man's real nature, the other desires being foreign to that nature. We look at others; think that they are more happy, would find out the cause, grow unreal and imitative. Ignorance makes us think others more happy, others think that we are more happy. A woman told me that she was dissatisfied with her daughter-in-law, but thought her neighbour happy with hers. I laughed and told her that I had heard the same story in the same language from her neighbour.

16. The highest form of detachment is the automatic renunciation of the three qualities, the result of Self-experience.

The quality of ignorance is superseded by the quality of passion, the quality of passion by that of purity, the quality of purity attained, it is difficult to renounce it. It gives a more unmixed pleasure than the other qualities, but creates more attachment. You can rise above

27

ignorance and passion with the help of purity, but you cannot rise above purity without the help of purity. That is the greatest struggle, the greatest achievement, the greatest renunciation.

17. Sampradnyāta Samādhi is that condition of conscious illumination, where mind is mixed up with consciousness of sentiment (sawitarka) or consciousness of discrimination (sawichāra) or consciousness of joy (sānanda) or consciousness of personality (sāsmita).

Meditation on nature begins with the meditation on her form, meditation on God begins with the meditation on His form. Meditation on nature or God without form, though not impossible, is extremely difficult; for we meditate with the help of mind, which Indian philosophy considers material (prakriti), though the object of our meditation be immaterial. When mind meditates on a beloved form of God, when the yôgi sees his God in form, talks with him, walks with him, argues with him, he gets attached to the form, he feels pain when the form disappears, he feels joy when it appears again, he is miserable when he gets no message, happy when he gets a message. The mind is pure, the form is pure, the relation is pure, but though pure it is still a sentiment, and all sentiment is weakness, bondage. When the yôgi controls that sentiment, he goes beyond it, becomes free. The same rule applies to meditation on nature, the more the yôgi meditates upon the form, the more he is attached to it; he realises the beauty, bounty, felicity of nature, but clings to it. In his heart of hearts he knows that all form is material, hence perishable; that the Self is beyond all form; yet he finds detachment difficult. He tries to reach the elements of nature, then tries to find out the one element that manifests itself in various forms, the root. Ultimately he finds that the material root is perishable. This process, this discrimination, goes on till he attains Self, the real root of nature. In all these various stages of meditation the yôgi enjoys inexpressible joy, at times he is carried away by his joy, the consciousness that he is enjoying is still there, because his personality refuses to leave him; though this personality is divested of the elements of passion and ignorance, still it maintains its individuality, refuses to merge into the all-embracing Impersonal. The yôgi is attached to his personal God, prides himself in being his devotee, his son, dedicates his life to him, sings his glory, enjoys his sense of duality, refuses to merge himself into his God, refuses to become God. God initiates him into this last stage, when the yôgi says: 'I am Spirit, the personal Self is the impersonal Self', leaves all for God, lives there forever. All these four conditions of illumination lead to unmixed conscious illumination which is final.

I met a yôgi who ridiculed the idea of God, maintained that there was nothing at the root of this world, that when man attains this nothingness he finds liberation. There mind becomes still, desire goes away. He thought that illumination was a negative condition, that we should begin with discrimination (buddhi), sift the good from the evil, the eternal from the non-eternal. He worked by elimination, attained the condition that he sought. He had great powers, consequently a great following, but when he died, his following melted away, for none believed in his philosophy, though all believed in his powers, all tried to turn them to their own advantage. He belonged to a dying doctrine. His body suffered great tortures in the end, he lost control of his mind, died a wreck.

I met yôgis who pinned their faith on Hatha-yôga, yôga based on the control of breath, as opposed to Rāja-yôga of Patanjali, based on the control of mind. The former tries to control mind through the control of breath, the latter tries to control breath through the control of mind. I met many who practised Hatha-yôga as a stepping stone to Rāja-yôga, but the few who were mere Hatha-yôgis had great powers, strong healthy bodies and immense vanity. So long as they were in the Hatha-yôga Samādhi, their minds were at rest, but as soon as they came out, their minds revolted. They were generally amenable to praise; and some more worldly than average worldly men.

That was the chief reason why I lost faith in Hatha-yôga. The Hatha-yôgi takes great care of his body, keeps it clean inside and outside, devotes so much time to it that he gets fond of it. The attachment grows with his years, grows still more when the powers come, when he becomes famous and people praise him, grows beyond all bounds. Body is the foundation of his spiritual life and he finds himself buried in it. No wonder if he finds it difficult to conquer his sentiment, go beyond discrimination, forget his joy, lose his personality. The Rāja-yôgi tries to ignore his personality, the Hatha-yôgi tries to develop it. The Rāja-yôgi knows that the mind once controlled, controls everything, that control of breath leads only to a temporary control of mind, that mind is more powerful than breath.

The yôgi is not always at fault, when he fails to go beyond a certain step. It is natural that when a certain step is attained, he feels inclined for rest, examines the ground he has covered, thinks of the ground he has yet to cover, enjoys the more perfect joy that he has found. Every new condition brings its own satisfaction, its more perfect joy, and the yôgi is tired after his journey. But if he prolong his rest too much, it grows on him, he refuses to move; the instruments through which he has been working, his body and his mind, are perfectly satisfied with what they have achieved, he forgets that there is still more perfect joy to come, he may even fail to understand the difference between the degrees of joy that he feels. He understands the difference between the joy that ignorance brings, the joy that passion brings, the joy that purity brings, but he fails to understand different degrees of joy that purity brings. He knows no standard by which to measure it except his

31

own, and every mind has its limitations. Then his master, who knows everything, comes to his rescue, tells him what to do. At times when I was in meditation I experienced extraordinary joy, felt so happy, hours passed like a second, but when I woke up, my master told me that I was not in Samādhi, but in deep sleep.

In the ordinary waking condition, the mind holds the image or object selected for meditation with great difficulty; in Sushupti, the best form of dreamless sleep, sometimes called unconscious Samādhi, the image is fixed; the thinker, the thinking, the thought are one; the meditations have reached their climax and are still; the sculptor, the marble block, are gone, but the statue remains. Presently the sleeper awakens, remembering nothing except perhaps his happiness. In the dreaming condition upon the other hand, the Self is there, there is constant change of image, dramatisation. The devotee may obtain his first instruction in dreams; the master or the God speaks, is visible; and the devotee so great his sense of sanctity, may awake crying out 'I have been in Samādhi'. But true Samādhi is the renewal of the waking condition, at a higher level; consciousness is now unbroken, and can at the will of the yôgi, know past present and future; be present at different places, or think in several streams of thought simultaneously; nothing of necessity is distant, whether in time or space; but this experience may last for a moment only; there is always an effort not to sink into Sushupti, the yôgi is upon the razor's edge.

Whether the sleeper is in Sushupti, is plunged in consciousness, but himself unconscious, or dreaming perhaps what he will forget on waking, his mind lies open to his master.

The classical enumeration of these conditions is in Māndookya-Upanishad. Patanjali examines only the different stages or steps of Samādhi.

The power of knowledge is great, the power of control of knowledge is greater. Spiritual life begins with control; you can get control by practice only. So long as mind is limited, the joy it can enjoy is limited; as soon as it merges itself into the Self, which is unlimited, the joy it can enjoy is unlimited. The problem is how to control the individual limited mind and dissolve it in the universal unlimited mind; that solved, the problem of life is solved, the individual gets his freedom.

I met a yôgi who was a great musician, another who was a great singer, both meditated on the inner music, listened to it day and night, but failed to control that pleasure and lead a normal life. One forgot that he had a body, forgot all that he should have remembered, somebody had to say 'Time to take food'; 'Time to go to the privy.'

When the yôgi moves in his spritual light, he forgets the faces of his nearest and dearest, when he listens to the inner music, he does not recognise the voices of others, when the taste of the tongue develops, all foods taste alike, when he smells perfume of all kinds, he does not appreciate the perfume of flowers, when extraordinary sensations arise in the body, he loses the sense of touch; yet all these are limited, though more perfect pleasures, the yôgi has to go beyond them all. So long as the yôgi fails to control pleasure, fails to control power, he fails to attain the final condition. As soon as he succeeds, he attains.

Miracles always happen, sometimes they are performed at the will of the yôgi, at others they happen without the knowledge of the yôgi. Miracles are not a dial that measures the condition of the yôgi. To measure him, find out whether he is the slave or the master of power. If he is the one, he is doomed; if he is the other, no one can question him. But to find out a yôgi, you must be a yôgi.

When the yôgi is playing into the hands of power, he does great evil. The idea of doing good is born with man. When the yôgi begins to do good, he may lose sense of proportion, lose the sight of his goal, be carried away by personal vanity, hanker after fame which all men call a bauble, deceive himself, deceive the world. I knew a yôgi, the disciple of a great master, who achieved great power, soothed the savage, healed the sick, led an austere life, but succumbed to fame. He gave the same prescription to a man with piles and to a man with phthisis, and both were cured. But his vanity ruined him. His master watched him, knew that he rebelled, guarded him when the time of death came. He repented, refused food and drink for days, meditated on his master, refused to meet anyone else and passed away in peace.

18. Asampradnyāta Samādhi is that unmixed condition of conscious illumination, where by constant renunciation of all knowledge, mind retains past impressions only.

So long as the personality is there, so long as the yôgi is carried away by the joy of meditation, he is in the snare of the sense, and may fall into the hands of powers that are the automatic result of his meditation. The yôgi is attached to his body, temptation is too strong. When he uses these powers his meditation fails; the more he is praised, the more does he exploit his spiritual powers, the more do people exploit him. All know the havoc of earthly power, but that of spiritual power is greater. If the yôgi remembers his vow of renunciation and renounces his spiritual knowledge, he is safe; if not, he travels the path over again. Worldly power is intoxicating; spiritual power is more intoxicating; but when the yôgi refuses to be drawn into it, his mind refuses to move, it refuses to love and hate, accepts what comes to it without effort, as the result of past karma. There is no new desire, no new fuel to feed the fire, the last embers are fast dying out, reduced to cold ashes, the last impressions on the mind die out, and the mind finds its rest in Self, dissolves itself in Self, loses its identity, loses its personality, becomes Self itself.

19. They who have lost attachment to body or have merged in nature, attain this condition when they are born again.

They who meditate on the material elements, completely identify themselves with those elements, and they who have lost all physical attachment, they attain Asampradnyāta Samādhi, but as they have not found the Self, they inherit that Samādhi. They are not free from life and death, because the impressions are still there.

20. But others have to attain it through faith, effort, recollection, concentration, discrimination.

They who have not earned it in their past lives, have to make their effort in the present. Some people attain miraculous power when they are young, while old men who have tried all their life, have hardly got any. The former inherited it as a legacy from their previous life, the latter have just found the path. A man of seventy came one day, with a tale of misery. He was born in a rich noble family, had everything that he wanted, but felt dissatisfied, renounced everything, stayed in the forest as a hermit for forty years, but had failed to awaken his kundalinee, and would die without success. He had very nearly lost his faith, but was restored to it. Through faith comes the energy that sustains the effort, through faith man remembers his goal, through faith he remembers his own experience and the experience of others; without faith he must make the same experiments over again, wasting time and energy. Concentration centres all the forces of mind on one object only to the detriment of others, once the knowledge of that object is attained, you discriminate between Self and non-Self, and this concentration is from faith.

21. Success is immediate where effort is intense.

22. Success varies according to whether the effort is mild, moderate or intense.

The degree of intensity with which the yôgi makes his effort gives him immediate or remote success. Unless his past karma intervenes, success generally is immediate. If, however, the yôgi is sincere, if his effort is intense, the grace of God or of the master intervenes, and the past karma is either condoned or postponed. Faith in God and his master removes all obstacles.

23. Illumination is also attained by devotion to God.

24. God is the One unique Personality, untouched by desire, affliction, action or its result.

God, though without form, is with form too; He has

the power to take any form according to the wish of the devotee. The yôgi who wants to meditate on a form, may choose any form he likes, concentrate on it, and solve his problem. Generally, form means desire, desire means action, action creates happiness or pain, happiness or pain creates a long chain of action in return; but God, though with a form, is not affected by desire and consequently is untouched by action and its result. If man wants to go beyond all desire, all action, he should meditate on one who is beyond all desire, all action; if man wants to go beyond all happiness and misery, he should meditate on God.

25. In Him lies the seed of omniscience.

He knows all, therefore love Him. He has got what we want. Though His attention be fixed upon another devotee, He knows what we want and where we are going.

26. He is the master of even the ancient masters, being beyond the limits of time.

27. His name is Ôm.

When you worship God with form, you must have a name for Him. The last word the yôgi hears before passing into the final condition of illumination is Ôm; when he passes out of it and comes to his sense again, the first word he hears is Ôm. Call Him what you please, but Ôm is His universal name.

28. Repeat it constantly; meditate on its meaning.

The meaning of Ôm is given in the Māndookya-Upanishad.

29. Devotion to God enlightens the soul, removes every obstacle.

30. Disease, lack of enthusiasm, doubt, irregularity, lethargy, yearning for sensual pleasure, hallucination, failure to attain a step, failure to maintain that step, are obstacles that distract the mind.

31. Pain, nervousness, sulkiness, irregular breathing, follow.

32. To destroy these, meditate on one object.

You have to take your mind from all other objects and concentrate on one only; if you worship the various forms of nature, worship one form only; if you worship many gods, worship one God only.

33. Mind attains peace by associating with the happy, pitying the miserable, appreciating the virtuous, and avoiding the vicious.

You have to think of good, instead of evil. The more you think of good, the more it will cling to you.

There is no necessity for a background of evil for your thought of good. It is waste of time to analyse what is almost everywhere; rather to forget it is sound wisdom.

34. Also by expulsion and retention of breath.

Breathing exercises, if carried on under the direct supervision of a competent teacher, would bring peace to the mind.

35. Mind attains peace, when meditation produces extra-ordinary sense-perceptions.

Meditation on the tip of the nose awakens the element of earth and creates extraordinary perfumes, meditation on the tip of the tongue awakens the element of water and creates extraordinary tastes, meditation on the sun or moon or stars awakens the element of light and creates extraordinary forms of beauty, meditation on Ôm or any other sacred word awakens the element of air and creates extraordinary forms of inner music, meditation on the form of God awakens the element of wind and creates extraordinary sensations of touch; they all bring conviction to the oscillating mind, and that conviction brings peace.

36. Or by meditation on the inner light that leads beyond sorrow.

You have to meditate on the flame that is always burning in your heart.

37. Or by meditation on saints who have attained desirelessness.

As you meditate, so you become. Meditate on power, you draw power; meditate on wealth, you draw wealth; meditate on saintliness, you become a saint. You may meditate on the masters of old who are immortal, or you may meditate on the living saints, you will obtain the same result. I have met people who have worshipped Lord Dattātreya, Lord Shiva, the Goddess Kālee, the sage Wyāsa, saint Dnyāneshwar, who flourished hundreds or thousands of years ago, and still they get their initiation from them.

38. Or by meditation on the knowledge gained through dream or sleep.

Many a time the spiritual call comes in a dream. The spiritual guide gives his instructions in a dream, and many spiritual doubts are solved in dreams. Through dreams, the immortals initiate their disciples. Or you can meditate on this world as the illusion of a dream or as the ignorance of sleep, only fit to be renounced.

39. Or by meditation on anything you will.

There is no end to things on which you can meditate. Meditate on earth, air, water, wind, light; meditate on sun, moon, stars; meditate on the wise, the beautiful, the virtuous; meditate on the tip of the nose, the tip of the tongue, the middle of the eyebrows; meditate on any form male or female; meditate on any god that you love; meditate on your own form as seen in a mirror; the form does not matter; it is always the power of meditation that matters.

40. Thus mind masters everything from the smallest to the greatest.

There is nothing which mind cannot grasp. Master your mind, master everything. When mind is mastered, it merges into the Self, the yôgi becomes master of himself, master of nature.

41. When mind's activity is controlled, illumination results, mind reflects the nature of either the seer, the seen, or the seeing, as pure crystal reflects the colour of whatever is placed on it.

When mind refuses to move, when it has nothing for discrimination, nothing to apportion between Self and non-Self, when by concentration it loses itself into the Self; the subject, the object, the instrument become one; the sculptor, the image in the mind, the statue, become one; the image disappears, the statue disappears, only the sculptor remains; the Self, the mind, the world become one; the world disappears, the mind disappears, only the Self remains.

In deep sleep only the statue remains; in Samādhi only the sculptor remains.

42. It is Sawitarka Samādhi, illumination with sentiment, when mind is still muddled with doubt as to word and its meaning.

43. It is Nirwitarka Samādhi, illumination

above sentiment, when doubt disappears, mind forgets itself, only meaning remains.

44. In the same way, illumination with discrimination, illumination above discrimination, illumination in regard to each of the finer objects can all be defined and described.

45. The finer objects end with the unmanifest seed.

The element of perfume is finer than earth, the element of taste is finer than water, the element of beauty is finer than light, the element of wind is finer than touch, the element of sound is finer than air, the element of personality is finer than all the previous elements, the element of the unmanifest where all objects come to an end, finer than the element of personality.

46. These are all types of illumination with seed.

Illumination with sentiment, above sentiment; with discrimination; above discrimination with joy; above joy; with personality, above personality; these are eight types of illumination with seed.

47. Illumination above discrimination, being pure, brings spiritual contentment.

In this condition the intellect, the discriminative faculty, has nothing to discriminate; and the mind is set at rest.

48. In this condition, the intellect becomes pregnant with truth.

49. Instead of knowledge gained through evidence and inference, it brings direct knowledge of objects and their meaning in its entirety.

Evidence of scriptures and of saints and prophets is no more necessary, the yôgi gets his own experience.

50. The impression remaining after this illumination excludes every other impression.

51. When even this has been suppressed, seedless Samādhi is attained.

Then 'Self stays in His native condition' (*Vide* Book 1, 3), the yôgi attains liberation.

II
Practice

II
Practice

1. Austerity, study, devotion to God, constitute practical yôga.

Continence, control of the desire for food, control of tongue by speaking the truth or observing silence, indifference to heat and cold, service of the master, constitute austerity. Studying the Wedas and the Upanishads, pondering over their meaning, repeating Ôm, constitute study.

2. The aim is to attain Illumination and to destroy afflictions.

3. Ignorance, egoism, desire, aversion, fear, are afflictions.

4. Ignorance is the cause, the others are the effects, whether they are dormant, weak, suppressed or aggravated.

Egoism creates desire, creates aversion, aversion brings on retaliation, man lives in fear of death, the main weakness of flesh.

5. Ignorance thinks of the perishable as imperishable, of the pure as impure, of the

painful as pleasurable, of the non-Self as Self.

6. Egoism is the identification of the Seer with the limitations of the eye.

As well as the identification of the Hearer with the limitations of the ear, the Taster with the limitations of the tongue, the Smeller with the limitations of the nose, the Toucher with the limitations of the skin, the Thinker with the limitations of the mind.

7. Desire is longing for pleasure.

8. Aversion is recoiling from pain.

9. Fear is that constant natural terror of death, that is rooted even in the minds of the learned.

Fear of death is constant in the mind, and as desire and aversion are the result of some experience in the past, so is the fear of death the result of dying in the past.

10. The finer afflictions disappear as mind disappears in illumination.

11. The grosser afflictions disappear through meditation.

As the grosser layers of dirt dissolve in soap, finer layers disappear when the linen is thrown into boiling water; the grosser afflictions dissolve into meditation, the finer afflictions disappear in illumination.

12. Karma, whether fulfilled in present or future life, has its root in afflictions.

13. So long as the root is present, karma remains, creates re-birth, governs its fulfilment and duration of fulfilment.

The laws of karma are mysterious, it is difficult to find out whether the karma that man is fulfilling in this life is the result of his past or present, for while fulfilling the past, he is creating new karma for the future, and intense karma whether it is virtuous or vicious brings an immediate result. The karma created in one body may be fulfilled in another body, in another life; a portion is fulfilled in life, another portion fulfilled in another.

14. It creates pleasure or pain as it springs from virtue or vice.

15. To the discriminating mind, all karma is painful, for pain follows them all in the end, they cause irritation, leave impressions behind, create the conflict between the three Qualities.

16. Future misery is to be avoided.

The past karma is dead, it deserves to be forgotten, what is done cannot be undone; the present must be fulfilled, that is the law of karma, there is no escape; but the future is in our hands.

17. The link between the Seer and the seen, creates misery, is to be broken.

18. Purity, passion, ignorance, constitute the seen; element and sense its modifications; enjoyment and liberation its aim.

19. Gross, fine, manifest, unmanifest, are the four conditions of the three qualities.

Earth, fire, water, air, wind; seeing, hearing, tasting, smelling, speaking; tongue, hands, feet, organ of generation, organ of excretion, and mind; constitute the gross conditions. Taste, touch, sound, smell, beauty, personality, constitute the fine conditions. Intellect, the discriminative faculty, constitutes the manifest condition, and seed of nature the unmanifest condition of qualities.

20. The Seer is sight itself, but though untainted, appears as if tainted through the vagaries of the intellect.

It is the colouring of the intellect that creates the taint.

21. The seen exists for the Seer alone.

The seen is the playing ground of the Seer, it has no independent existence.

22. The seen is dead to him who has attained liberation, but is alive to others, being common to all.

If one man gets his liberation, it does not follow that the world becomes free. Every man has to struggle for himself. Because men have the same desires, they have the same playing ground.

23. The Seer and the seen are linked together that the real nature of each may be known.

24. The cause of this link is ignorance.

25. No ignorance, no link. The breaking of the link reveals the independence of the Seer.

26. Unwavering discrimination between Self and non-Self, destroys ignorance.

Discrimination between Self and non-Self, the eternal and non-eternal, the cause and its effect, carried to its logical end, brings in revelation.

27. The enlightenment that comes to a yôgi at the last step is seven-fold.

(1) The yôgi knows what renunciation means, (2) renounces what is to be renounced, (3) sifts the cause from the effect, (4) attains liberation, (5) is satisfied with the result, (6) the qualities are dissolved, (7) the aim of life is fulfilled.

28. Impurities having been washed away by the practice of meditation, the light of knowledge shines till discrimination is complete.

29. Yama, Niyama, Āsana, Prānāyāma, Pratyāhāra, Dhāranā, Dhyāna, Samādhi, are eight steps of yôga.

30. Refusal of violence, refusal of stealing,

refusal of covetousness, with telling truth and continence, constitute the Rules (yama).

Refusal of violence is love for all creatures, refusal of stealing is love for one's neighbours, refusal of covetousness is maintaining the dignity of oneself, truth-telling is maintaining the dignity of society, continence is not exploiting women for one's own pleasure.

All life is sacred, all life is one; no one has a right to question the sacredness of another, no one has a right to commit violence against another. The yôgi who wants to find the unity of life, should not break that unity. Thought, word, or deed, unconsciously willed, may create misery. Men differ in temperament, character, environment, but they all stand on the one rock of Self, and when man commits violence on man, he commits it on himself; he may not know the law, but the law will claim him, if not here, certainly hereafter.

It is for self-preservation, the natural instinct in man, that violence is forbidden.

The same principle applies to stealing. Whatever belongs to man, belongs to him, because he has earned it, may be in his past life, nobody else has a right to it. Stealing is physical while covetousness is mental. The yôgi who wants to control his mind, should control his desire, his passion, his greed, that he may not steal in his heart. When man refuses to covet, refuses to steal, in any sense refuses to be violent, he speaks the truth.

Mental energy is the product of seed, hence the necessity of conserving what gives the yôgi the power to concentrate.

31. These are sacred vows, to be observed, independent of time, place, class or occasion.

32. Purity, austerity, contentment, repetition of sacred words, devotion to God, constitute the Regulations (niyama).

33. If wrong sentiments disturb, cultivate right thoughts.

34. Think that wrong actions, violence and the like, whether committed caused or abetted, whether provoked by anger avarice or infatuation, whether they seem important or unimportant, obstruct meditation, bring endless ignorance and misery.

35. When non-violence is firmly rooted, enmity ceases in the yôgi's presence.

36. When truth is firmly rooted, the yôgi attains the result of action without acting.

Whatever the yôgi says becomes true, his word is law.

37. When non-stealing is firmly rooted, riches are attained.

38. When continence is firmly rooted, the yôgi becomes potent.

39. When non-covetousness is firmly rooted the yôgi knows his past, present, future.

40. When purity is attained, the yôgi shrinks from his body, avoids the touch of others.

41. He attains as well clarification of intellect, cheerfulness of mind, subjugation of sense, power of concentration, that fit him for Self-experience.

42. Contentment brings supreme happiness.

43. Austerity destroys impurity, awakens physical and mental powers.

He can take any form he likes, attains clairvoyance, clairaudience.

44. Repetition of sacred words brings you in direct contact with the God you worship.

45. Illumination is attained by devotion to God.

46. Āsana (Posture) implies steadiness and comfort.

47. It requires relaxation and meditation on the Immovable.

48. Then opposing sensations cease to torment.

Sensations like pleasure and pain, heat and cold, honour and dishonour.

54

49. The next step is Prānāyāma (Control of Breath), the cessation of exhalation and inhalation.

50. Exhalation, inhalation, cessation of breath, may be short or long, according to length, duration and number of breaths.

51. A fourth method of breathing is that which is determined by a uniform external or internal measure.

Outward breath can be measured by fingers; inward breath, by its contact with various nerve-centres (chakrams).

52. Then the cloud that obscures light, melts away;

53. And mind becomes fit for attention.

54. Pratyāhāra is the Restoration of sense to the original purity of mind, by renouncing its objects.

55. Then follows the complete subjugation of sense.

Yama, Niyama, Āsana, Pranāyāma, Pratyāhāra, are the five steps that constitute the outer phase of yôga. Yama, Niyama are rules and regulations to govern the body and the mind, Āsana governs the body, and through that, the mind. There are many postures, six more important than the others. Their theory and practice have been developed to a great extent by

Hatha-Yôga. The yôgi of that school takes substantial food, takes it at regular intervals, eats no meat, and practises the postures. These postures have been incorporated in the Rāja-Yôga system and I have not met a yôgi who has not practised one or two, especially the Siddhāsana or Padmāsana. In the earlier stages they practise a few others, to gain physical fitness and immunity from disease. But during my travels in India, to my horror and amazement, I found caricatures of these postures, and it is no wonder that when the tradition is being lost, people pin their faith in books which give inaccurate or inadequate accounts. These caricaturing postures do not harm those who practise them for physical fitness, every posture for a minute or two, but they do incalculable harm to those who want to keep a posture for three hours, one Prahar at a stretch—least time when spiritual results are aimed at—for, comfort and ease are the essentials of any posture. The yôgi will find that every forty-eight minutes—two Ghatikās—a painful sensation or pang, travels through the body, and he is tempted to give up the posture, but if he sticks to it through three such pangs, he feels pain no more. The same thing applies to the breathing exercises. Unless they are studied under the guidance of a competent teacher, they are dangerous.

People forget that Yama and Niyama form the foundation, and unless it is firmly laid, they should not practise postures and breathing exercises. In India and

Europe, I came across some three hundred people who suffered permanently from wrong practices, the doctors on examination found that there was nothing organically wrong and consequently could not prescribe.

Yama, Niyama, Āsana, Prānāyāma, all lead up to Pratyāhāra. The aim of the first four is to awaken the power of the kundalinee, as a prelude to Pratyāhāra, Pratyāhāra itself but the prelude to concentration. There are three nerves, Idā, Pingalā, Sushumnā, the first two passing through either side of the spinal cord, their passage being clear; but the Sushumnā passage that runs between the two is closed, and unless it is opened for the kundalinee, no achievement in yôga is possible. Hence the attention of the yôgi is centred on the kundalinee.

I asked a great Mahātmā what would awaken the kundalinee and he said: 'Renunciation, Renunciation, Renunciation', and I found it true. I met some Hatha-Yôgis who through postures and breathing exercises awakened the kundalinee, but as soon as they left their meditative life, the passage closed again. It is the inner fire, the serpentine fire, as it is called, that leads a man to liberation, that makes the mind fit for concentration, and the body fit to sustain the weight of the higher spiritual powers.

It is a terrifying experience when the kundalinee is awakened. The first day the fire was kindled in me, I thought I was dying, the whole body was, as it were, on fire, mind was being broken to pieces, the bones were being hammered, I did not understand what was happening. In three months, I drank gallons of milk and clarified butter, ate leaves of two nimba trees till they were left without a single leaf, searched everywhere for mudrā leaves and devoured those insipid things. During that period, I could not sit in any posture, I could not stand, I used to lie down on my bed and repeat the name of Lord Dattātreya. I know of cases where the fire was not brought under control for six or eight months; one mahātmā told me that he used to sit under a cold water tap for eight hours every day. There is no danger to life, unless the rules and discipline are disregarded; it is only an act of purification, through which every one must go if he wants to attain.

III
Powers

III
Powers

1. Attention fixed upon an object is Dhāranā.

The object may be the tip of the nose, the middle of the eyebrows, the sun, the moon, the pole-star, the feet or the eyes of your favourite image of God.

2. Union of mind and object is Dhyāna.

When the mind becomes one with its object, refuses to think of another, the condition is Dhyāna.

3. Samādhi is that condition of illumination where union as union disappears, only the meaning of the object on which the attention is fixed being present.

In Dhāranā, the attention upon an object is disturbed; in Dhyāna, the attention is not disturbed, but the consciousness of the thinker, the thinking and the object of thought are present; in Samādhi, the thinker, the thinking, the separate object, go away, only the object, transformed by and transparent to thought, remains.

4. The three together (attention, union, illumination) form (Samyama) Concentration.

5. Successful concentration is direct knowledge.

6. Concentration is necessary to mount the various steps.

To mount the steps of sentiment and discrimination, joy and personality; to travel from the grossest to the finest.

7. Attention, union, illumination, are more internal than the preceding five steps. (*Vide* Book II, 29.)

8. But they are external, compared with seedless Samādhi.

9. At every moment distractions and impressions of distractions lessen, control and impressions of control increase, until mind clings to the condition of control.

The forces of attachment and detachment simultaneously work on the mind, a constant fight goes on between worldly pleasures and spiritual pleasures, with the help of spiritual pleasures the yôgi controls the worldly pleasures, with the help of renunciation he controls the spiritual pleasures, till he attains the seedless Samādhi.

10. When the impressions of control prevail, mind flows peacefully.

11. When mind rejects all objects but one, illumination results.

When mind refuses to hunt after new objects of pleasure, is satisfied with one, gets there all it wants, is convinced that the world has nothing superior to give, it finds its rest.

12. It is the result of concentration that mind's attitude towards the object of concentration remains the same, to-day as yesterday.

It naturally follows that it will be the same in the future. Thus the three divisions of time, past present future, disappear, and time becomes one.

13. In the same way, the three-fold modifications of element and sense into form, age, and condition can be explained.

In the beginning, the forces of the mind are scattered, the yôgi tries to knit them together, tries to fix his attention on one object, to leave all others, succeeds in uniting his mind with that object, ultimately finds that both are finally dissolved in the Self. In the same way, element and sense lose their form. There is the clay, the potter reduces it to fine powder, all particles separate from one another, he joins them by some binding material like water, gives it the shape of a vessel, bakes it, uses it, until it is broken, when it is reduced to clay again. In all these stages, it was always clay, nothing but clay, only the form changed. Time is divided into three divisions, which, when reduced, mean only one undivided time. It is all one road, the part of the road that we have travelled, is called past; the part of the road that we are travelling, is called present; the part of the road that we have to travel is called future. In the same way, age determines childhood, youth, old age; but in reality there is no age, as there is no time and no form. There is distraction, there is attention; the two fight; concentration is the result. There is ignorance (Tamas), there is passion (Rajas), there is purity (Satwa), the three fight; they have fought before, they are fighting now, they will fight hereafter; in the case of the yôgi, he controls them all, attains illumination, it is a fight to the finish. Those who do not carry the fight to a finish are born again and again, they talk of here and hereafter, they talk of past present and future, childhood youth and age.

14. Substance is that which is uniform in the past present and future.

The day which we call to-day, will to-morrow become yesterday; to-morrow will become to-day after twenty-four hours. To-day it is clay, to-morrow it takes the shape of a vessel, the day after it becomes clay again; it is clay all along; it is the substance that remains uniform, though it takes various shapes.

15. Different modifications of substance are due to different orders of sequence.

16. Concentrate on the above three-fold modifications; know past and future.

The sage Bhrigu worked out sometime in the past, the horoscopes of thousands of men, some alive to-day, some yet to be born. I saw my own horoscope, carved on palm leaves, written in Samskrit, giving an account of my past as well as present life. There are various copies of this collection of horoscopes; I know of one which is at Benāres, I saw another which belonged to a pundit from Malabār. It is called Bhrigu-Samhitā. Generally three lives are described, or rather one life in relation to the past and the future life.

17. Concentrate separately on the word, the meaning and the object, which are mixed up in common usage; understand the speech of every creature.

When we utter the word 'elephant', we find that the word, the meaning and the object are mixed up; the word lives in air, the meaning lives in mind, the elephant lives by itself.

18. Concentrate on the impressions of the past; know past lives.

19. Concentrate on another's mind; know that mind.

20. You cannot know its contents unless you concentrate on those contents.

The Mahātmā knows everything, it is not always that he is willing to expose himself and give his knowledge to others. In worldly matters, he is generally silent, they do not mean anything to him; in spiritual matters he gives you his knowledge, provided you have sufficient faith and receptivity. When I did not put a direct question to a Mahātmā, I got the answer, though it was directed to no one in particular.

21. Concentrate on the form of your body, suspend the power of another to see it; and as the light of his eye cannot reach you, become invisible.

When I went with a friend to Nāsik, a holy place of pilgrimage, in search of a relation of his, who had become a monk without the permission of his wife, and searched every cottage and hermitage, we were told by a hermit to wait at the entrance of a temple for a Swāmi who went there every evening; if we were lucky he would answer our question. We waited and saw the Swāmi, saluted him; he went into the temple, offered his prayers, came out; we followed him but he disappeared into the air to our utter amazement. Our question was too insignificant and too worldly.

I was with my Master, we were returning to Bombay from Viramgaon, he in the first class and I in the third. At Dādar, I got down, packed up his bedding, went to my compartment again. Grant Road came, we were to get down, I got down, moved from one end of the train to another, once, twice, thrice, failed to find my Master's compartment. I rubbed my eyes, pinched my arm, there was nothing wrong with me, I was not dreaming, and very nearly cried. I prayed to my Master not to test me more; immediately my Master placed his hand on my shoulder and asked me where I had been so long! I smiled, he laughed, and said, 'Come along, the porter is ready with the luggage.' The little service that I rendered to my Master created vanity, and this was the lesson. What man can serve a Mahātmā? It is the privilege of the Mahātmā to serve him.

In the same way, spoken words are hidden from persons not intended to hear them.

22. Concentrate on immediate or future karma; know the time and cause of death.

23. Concentrate on friendship, mercy, joy; excel in them.

24. Concentrate on strength like that of the elephant; get that strength.

25. Concentrate on inner Light; know the fine, the obscure, the remote.

26. Concentrate on the Sun; know the world.

Whatever is in man, is in the Sun; whatever is in the Sun, is in man.

27. Concentrate on the Moon; know the planets.

In Kashmere I was introduced by a scientist to an unassuming young man, sitting under a chinār tree, smoking the hukkā, the hubble-bubble, who was a great saint. He knew not a word of any language but his own, Marāthi, and when I asked the scientist about him, he said he asked him questions about astronomy, about Sun, Saturn, Jupiter, Mars, and found he knew everything that a modern scientist knew, and much more which the scientist has yet to find out.

28. Concentrate on the pole-star; know the motions of stars.

29. Concentrate on the navel; know the organism of the body.

30. Concentrate on the hollow of the throat; go beyond hunger and thirst.

31. Concentrate on the nerve called Koorma; attain steadiness.

32. Concentrate on the Light in the head; meet the Masters.

The Masters are the immortals. The Master instructs the pupil in the beginning through dreams, sometimes only the voice is heard, without any form uttering it; at others he appears in dreams in the form of a holy man and gives instructions; later on when the pupil is advanced, he gives his name and appears in his natural form. A time comes when the yôgi yearns to meet him face to face and he meets him; he meets all of them if he wants to.

Some of the Masters who long ago entered a cave alive in the presence of thousands, are still there; they draw people to them, show them the Light. I know some instances in the past which are recorded, some in the present as well.

33. Concentrate on intelligence; know everything.

34. Concentrate on the heart; know every mind.

The yôgi knows every mind along with its desires.

35. Sensation is the result of the identification of Self and intellect; they radically differ from each other, the latter serving the cause of the former; concentrate on the real Self; know that Self.

Those who forget the Self and attend to intellect, thinking that intellect is everything, forget the host, attend to the servant. Self is the cause, intellect only an instrument. You can know the Self through Self only. Who can know the knower, how can he know the knower, except through himself?

36. Then follows enlightenment; the sublimation of the sense of sight, smell, touch, taste, hearing.

Knowledge of the fine, the obscure, the remote, follows; knowledge of the past, the present, the future; of what the eye does not see, the nose does not smell, the skin does not touch, the tongue does not speak, the ear does not hear.

37. These powers of knowledge are obstacles to illumination; but illumination apart, they bring success.

They have their value so far as this world is concerned, but they obstruct the progress of the soul so far as its liberation is concerned. The power they give is an encumbrance, unless it is under control.

38. When the cause of bondage is removed, the yôgi can by knowledge of the nervous system, concentrate his mind upon the body of another and enter into it.

The nature of mind is to go anywhere and everywhere, but it is bound down to one body because of its limited and particular desires; when mind gets free from that bondage, it can enter into any living or dead body, and thus fulfil its past karma.

39. By concentration on Udāna, living fire, the yôgi remains unaffected in water, in swamps, or amid thorns; leaves his body at will.

Recently the case of a yôgi sitting with crossed legs floating on water for three days was reported in Indian papers, cases of walking on fire happen every year, I know the case of a yôgi who always walked with bare feet, thorns did not prick them, snow did not chill them. The yôgi can enter into or take any form he likes, and when his karma is exhausted, he can disintegrate his body at his pleasure.

40. By concentration on the Samāna, living fire, the yôgi creates a halo of light about him.

The yôgi's 'aura' is particularly bright.

41. By concentrating on the relation between air and ear, the yôgi hears the divine message.

The ear depends upon air for hearing, the eye depends upon light for seeing, the nose depends upon earth for smelling, the tongue depends on water for tasting, the skin depends upon wind for touching.

42. By concentrating on the relation between air and body, and identifying himself with light things like cotton wool, the yôgi moves in the sky.

I saw a Mahātmā, sitting in the Siddhāsana posture with crossed legs, hanging in the air. The same Mahātmā went to Benāres from Nāgpur with the speed of thought through air and dissolved his body in the Ganges. A fuller account is given in *An Indian Monk*, page 37.

43. By concentrating on the involuntary activity of mind, completely unconscious of the

body, the veil that obscures light is drawn aside.

In the beginning, when the yôgi sends his mind out in the world, he is conscious of his body; but by constant practice, his mind goes out, is not conscious of his body, wills, acts, brings about certain results. There is nothing to obstruct his will; the way becomes clear.

44. By concentrating on the grossness, fineness, nature, relation, and purpose of elements, their conquest is attained.

45. Then follows the power to take any form, big or small; a sound body which nothing can destroy.

The chief powers are eight: (1) the power to take the smallest form, (2) the power to take the biggest form, (3) the power to take the lightest form, (4) the power to touch anything, (5) the power to control anything, (6) the power to create anything, (7) the power to penetrate anything, (8) the power to bring about anything. The minor powers are innumerable. The yôgi's body becomes so sound that heat or cold cannot kill it; the elements have no jurisdiction over it.

46. Soundness of body means beauty, grace, strength, hardness like adamant.

As Saint Tukārām said, the body of the yôgi becomes softer than wax and harder than adamant.

47. By concentrating on the activity, nature, individuality, relation, purpose of every sense, their conquest is attained.

48. Then the yôgi moves with the speed of thought, causes sense to work without body, conquers nature.

Many events in the history of the world are brought about by the will of the yôgi, which the world does not know and will never know.

49. Once the yôgi is convinced that Self and intellect are two, he masters the qualities, masters their results, knows everything.

50. Finally, by renouncing even these powers, the seed of bondage being destroyed, the yôgi attains liberation.

51. The yôgi should not be allured or wonderstruck by the courtship of celestial powers, lest he fall into the undesirable world again.

Liberation is eternal life, freedom from temporary life and death. The yôgi should not be surprised at things which happen, they may be the result of his conscious or unconscious will, he should renounce every claim to his powers, forget his personality, think

73

of Self, meditate on Self, dedicate everything to Self, wipe away every word written on the slate of his mind, enjoy his Self; otherwise he will find himself thrown once more into the vortex of birth and death.

52. Concentration on the present moment, the moment gone, and the moment to come, brings enlightenment, the result of discrimination.

The moment is the irreducible minimum; the second, the minute, the hour, the day, the month, the year, are the sum-total of moments. When the yôgi discriminates, throws away the grosser forms, meditates on the finer, he attains a stage where the finest thing cannot be reduced further in time and space. That stage brings knowledge.

53. It also brings knowledge of the difference between two similar objects, when that difference cannot be known by kind, character or locality.

All can understand the difference between a cow and a mare, they are two kinds of animals; all can understand the difference between a black cow and a white cow, they differ in one character; all can understand the difference between an Indian mango and an African mango, they differ in the locality where they were grown; but when things are so similar that an ordinary man finds it difficult to find out the difference, the yôgi succeeds in doing it.

54. Such knowledge, the result of discrimination, extended at the same time to all objects, under all conditions, leads to liberation.

55. When intellect becomes as pure as Self, liberation follows.

IV
Liberation

IV

Liberation

1. Powers are either revealed at birth, or acquired by medicinal herbs, or by repetition of sacred words, or through austerity, or through illumination.

Powers acquired in this life are revealed in the next. All know the healing qualities of herbs; only few know that some of them have the quality of awakening spiritual powers. I read so much about Jyotishmatee Kalpa in Samskrit books that I tried, with the help of two friends, to find out the prescription; we met only one yôgi who knew it by personal experience; after two years we had enough seed of Mālkāngnee to give us the necessary oil; this had to be mixed with the extracts of certain other herbs whose names I have forgotten; after six months the prescription was ready, we were to lie down in a cell for six months, with only sufficient air and light, never to stir out, live on milk and butter only, drink the Mālkāngnee mixture three times a day, observe strict silence; when I sought the permission of my father, it was refused and the plan was dropped.

Repeating Ôm or the name of the favourite God, awakens the powers.

2. The yôgi can transform himself into another life, gathering together the elements and character of that life.

The yôgi assembles the constituents of nature, earth, water, fire, wind, air, mind, personality, and fills them with the necessary combination of the three qualities, creating successive or simultaneous personalities, to fulfil his karma.

3. Elements work of their own accord, good and evil do not cause them to work, but act as implements only; water flows downwards naturally when the farmer removes obstacles in the way.

4. The yôgi provides minds for the bodies he creates through his personality.

5. Though the activities of such minds vary, the one original mind of the yôgi controls them all.

The yôgi thinks differently through different minds, acts differently through different bodies, but the original mind that controls them all, remains unaffected.

6. The controlling mind, born of illumination, remains unaffected by the contagion of desire.

When the yôgi creates different bodies to fulfil his past karma, his mind that is dissolved in his Self, remains dissolved, though the various minds that control the various bodies he creates, are endowed with particular desires, good and evil, according to his past karma.

7. The yôgi's karma is neither pure nor impure; that of others is pure, impure or mixed.

The worldly standard of purity and impurity does not apply to the yôgi; he is above law and custom.

8. From this three-fold karma desires spring up, that are helpful to its fulfilment.

9. Since recollections and impressions are the same, desires are awakened automatically, though separated by time, incarnation, country.

Action is the cause, recollections and impressions its effects. They work together, awaken the necessary desires, though the various actions were committed in different lives, at different times and in different countries.

The same soul is born in two different countries, he fights on behalf of one country against another in which he was previously born, pits one life against the life that went before it, his desire binds his actions, he is not bound by family or nationality.

10. Desires have no beginning.

Desire for life, follows aversion for death; aversion for death follows desire for life; desire for happiness, aversion for pain, follow each other in the same way. Life has no beginning, no end, there is only the emergence and mergence.

11. Desires are the aggregate result of ignorance and vanity, mind and the object of its hunt; they are absent when these are absent.

12. In reality, past and future exist as much as present; they are not seen because they exist on different planes.

If the past and future did not exist in reality, the yôgi could not have seen them through concentration; he does not create the past, he only sees it as it happened; he does not create the future, he only sees it as it will happen. Man does not see the past as he does not see the part of the road he has travelled, neither does he see the future as he does not see the part of the road he has yet to travel, because of his limited vision.

13. The present is manifest, the past and the future are obscure, but they all live in the Qualities.

They are manifestations of the combination of purity (Satwa), passion (Rajas), ignorance (Tamas); Qualities the cause, past present future the effect.

14. Though the Qualities are more than one, their material is one, their result is one.

Though the branches of the tree are many, the seed is one, the seed that causes the tree and the seed that is in the fruit of the tree.

15. Though the object is one, different minds see it differently.

Every object stands by itself, though different minds look at it differently. The husband sees a woman as his wife, the son sees her as his mother, the husband's mistress sees her as a rival, the hermit sees her as a danger, yet it is the same woman.

16. No object depends on one mind only; otherwise what becomes of it when that mind sees it no longer?

17. Object becomes known, when it is reflected in the mind; when it is not reflected, it remains unknown.

The object attracts the mind as the magnet attracts the needle, it transforms the mind, affects it constantly. Knowledge and ignorance are phases of the mind.

18. The activities of mind are known to the Self; for Self is the Lord, who remains unaffected.

There is nothing which Self does not know.

19. Mind does not shine by itself, being an object of perception.

Self is the Seer, the mind belongs to the seen.

20. Mind cannot at the same time know itself and any other object.

21. If we grant a second mind illuminating the first, we grant what is ridiculous; it would confuse memory.

We should have to grant innumerable minds, one to illuminate the other.

22. Though Self does not move, it is reflected in the mind, and when mind takes the form of that reflection, Self becomes conscious of sensation.

Unlimited consciousness of the Self, means joy beyond sensation, beyond pleasure and pain; but as soon as it is limited to the consciousness of the mind, sensation results, man oscillates between pleasure and pain.

23. The Seer and the seen are both reflected in the mind, hence it takes any conceivable form.

As water has no colour, it takes any colour that you mix it with; so mind has no form of its own, it takes any form.

24. The mind is coloured with innumerable desires, and as mind and desires work hand in hand, it follows that mind works to please some one else.

Mind is an agent working on behalf of its master.

25. He who sees clearly, refuses to identify mind with Self.

He finds that mind is not the doer, mind is not the knower, mind is not the enjoyer.

26. Intent on discrimination, his mind longs for liberation.

27. Sometimes in Illumination, impressions of the waking mind intervene.

The condition of Illumination is the condition of unlimited joy. Sometimes the limitations of waking mind shake the over-flowing joy.

28. They should be destroyed as afflictions are destroyed (Book II, 10–11).

29. When the yôgi attains final discrimination, renounces even that, he attains the condition called 'Rain-cloud of Divinity'.

The whole process of discrimination is the elimination of all limitations; when that is attained, the process itself is to be eliminated, as a man who lights the fire throws away the match. Nothing remains then to hinder the natural outpouring of divinity.

30. Then action and affliction come to an end.

The yôgi does not act though acting, he acts though not acting. When the seed of action is burnt, no affliction can touch him.

31. Mind without impurity and impediment, attains infinite knowledge; what is worth knowing in this world becomes negligible.

All knowledge, all power, belong to the yôgi; the world looks like a dream, a mirage, an illusion.

32. The procession of Qualities comes to an end; their purpose is fulfilled.

33. Procession means changes that occur from moment to moment, but seen only when that moment is gone.

The procession of cause and effect comes to a standstill; the procession of past and present becomes an eternal presence.

34. The dissolution of Qualities in their source, when nothing remains to be achieved, is liberation; the revelation of the power of Self, the foundation of the beauty of Self.

All doubts are dissolved, the problem of life is solved, the yôgi attains the goal, becomes free, for ever free.

Yogic Postures

Note. Hold your breath while doing a posture, begin to breathe when you complete it.

1. Siddhāsana

My Master's Favourite

Fold the left leg, set its heel against the peri-
neum, its sole closely fitting the right thigh;
then fold the right leg, set its heel against the
pubic bone, its sole closely fitting the left thigh;
lodge the testicles comfortably between the
heels; stretch your arms, rest them on your
knees. Sit erect.

2. Baddha-Padmāsana

Lotus-lock Posture

Fold your right leg, set its heel in the left groin with its sole turned up; fold your left leg, set its heel in the right groin with its sole turned up; both heels pressing the stomach. Then hook the toe of the left leg by the index finger of the left hand from the back, hook the toe of the right leg by the index finger of the right hand from the back. Sit erect.

3. Pashchimottānāsana

Folding Posture

Stretch your legs, keep them close; hook the toes with your index fingers, right by the right, left by the left, rest your head on the knees; do not bend them.

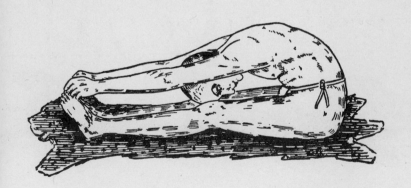

4. Bhujangāsana

Cobra Posture

Lie on your chest, relax; slowly raise your neck, then chest, then belly, with the dignity of the cobra.

5. Wipareeta Karanee

Inverted Posture

Place your head in the finger-lock, raise your trunk, then knees, then feet, stand erect on your head.

6. Matsyendrāsana

Master Matsyendra's Posture

Fold the right leg, keep its heel on the navel; fold the left leg, keep it to the right of the right thigh, the sole of the left foot lying flat on the carpet, hook the toe of the left foot by the index finger of the right hand, the right hand leaning on the left knee and keeping the left knee to its right; turn your left hand from the back and hold the heel of the right leg; keep neck and chest erect.